Michael

Go Home, Squirrel

Elspeth Campbell Murphy
Illustrated by Anne Kennedy

Chariot Books ™
David C Cook Publishing Co

Chariot Books™ is an imprint of David C. Cook Publishing Co.
David C. Cook Publishing Co., Elgin, Illinois 60120
David C. Cook Publishing Co., Weston, Ontario

GO HOME SQUIRREL
©1990 by Elspeth Campbell Murphy for text and Anne
Kennedy for illustrations

Book and cover design by Dawn Lauck

First Printing, 1990
Printed in Singapore
94 93 92 91 90 5 4 3 2 1

ISBN 1-55513-548-X
LC 88-62948

Michael was busy in the kitchen making snakes and pancakes out of clay. All of a sudden, he heard a loud CRASH!

"Michael!" called his mother from the living room. "What did you break?"

"Nothing," answered Michael, looking all around him in surprise. "Clay doesn't go CRASH."

Michael's mother and father rushed into the kitchen to see what Michael was up to. But the sounds weren't coming from there at all. They were coming from the family room. So Michael and his parents rushed into the family room, and—

—what a mess!

"Oh, no!" said Michael's mother.

"Who did this?" said Michael's father.

"A squirrel!" squealed Michael. "There's a squirrel in our house!"

And, sure enough, a wild little
squirrel was running all around
the room, knocking things over
and leaving sooty little paw prints
here, there, and everywhere.

Michael said, "What are you trying to do, squirrel? Break things and get me in trouble in my own house?"

Michael's mother laughed and said, "No, the poor little squirrel got in by mistake, and he is very scared to be in a people-house."

Michael's father said, "Michael, run and get the big broom from the garage."

Michael was glad to help, and he was back in half a minute.

Mother held the door open wide.
And with the broom, Father gently
nudged the little squirrel in the
right direction.

Michael said softly, "Go home,
squirrel. Go home to your own
house!"

Finally the little squirrel scampered out the door, across the lawn, and up the tree.

"Whew!" said Michael. "Back to his *own* house where he belongs."

"Exactly," said his mother. "God gave the squirrel just the right kind of home for squirrels."

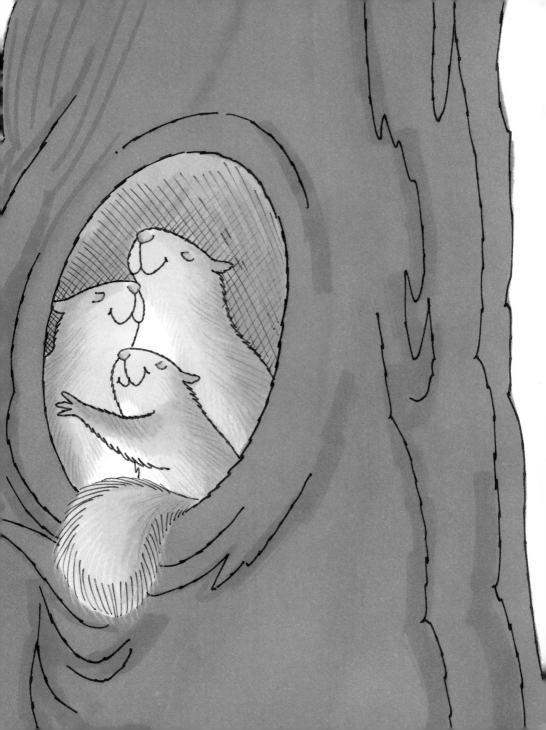

Michael said, "And you know what? God gave *me* just the right kind of home for *me*!"

Have you read these books about Michael?

The Big Surprise
Go Home, Squirrel
The Friendly Bear
The Big Red Truck

Look for all the Michael books at your local Christian bookstore.